Buffy THE VAMPIRE SLAYER™
Uninvited Guests

Buffy the Vampire Slayer™
Uninvited Guests

based on the television series created by
JOSS WHEDON

writer **ANDI WATSON**

"New Kid on the Block" co-written with
DAN BRERETON

penciller **HECTOR GOMEZ**

inker **SANDU FLOREA**

colorist **GUY MAJOR**

letterer **JANICE CHIANG**

These stories take place during Buffy the Vampire Slayer's second season.

Titan Books

publisher
MIKE RICHARDSON

editor
SCOTT ALLIE
with ADAM GALLARDO *and* BEN ABERNATHY

designer
KRISTEN BURDA

art director
MARK COX

special thanks to
DEBBIE OLSHAN AT FOX LICENSING,
CAROLINE KALLAS AND GEORGE SNYDER AT *BUFFY THE VAMPIRE SLAYER,*
AND DAVID CAMPITI AT GLASS HOUSE GRAPHICS.

PUBLISHED BY
TITAN BOOKS LTD,
144 SOUTHWARK ST.
LONDON SE1 0UP

JANUARY 2000
FIRST EDITION
ISBN: 1 - 84023 - 140 - 8

1 3 5 7 9 10 8 6 4 2

printed in canada

introduction
BY andi watson

Vampires. They're everywhere. Look around and you'll see vampire books, games, trading cards, Popsicles, mouse pads, TV shows and comics. Just when you think every vampire angle has been covered—you're right—it's been done to death! Pop culture is full of images of half (un-)dressed actresses chowing down on some loser's neck. Or another angsty guy in a frilly shirt following a similar po-faced routine. Unless he's a Vampire Cop, which calls for a change of uniform.

I can't deny the appeal of the genre; I'm not entirely innocent myself. I had Chinese-hopping-hockey-vampires in my own book, *Skeleton Key*, a while back. I guess I can't help but inject a little humor into the proceedings. Which may explain why Jamie S. Rich (the first editor on the series) gave me a call many moons ago to ask if I'd be interested in writing this *Buffy* book that Dark Horse was bringing out.

At that time the show hadn't reached Jolly Ol' England, but I had seen the movie. I'd warmed to the concept—*Heathers* meets *Dracula*—neato! And any movie with Luke Perry, a guy willing to play Krusty the Clown's despised half-brother, is okay by me. Horror has never been my thing, in fact the only horror I've experienced is the searing back pain felt by trying to lift one of the genre's best sellers off the shelf. I'd misspent my youth watching trashy teen movies, not trashy slasher flicks. And while I lacked an encyclopedic knowledge of horror shower scenes, I did know my Molly Ringwalds from my Ally Sheedys. All of which has held me in good stead since, to my surprise, I got the job. *Buffy* is all about being a teen. It's funny and ironic and has a very healthy amount of self-deprecation.

After all if you can't find humor in frilly shirts then you're missing out on life.

Andi
June '99

White Christmas

BAD MOVE.

GAH!

KSSH

UH, HI. THIS YOUR CAR?

MUH... MUH...

...SO I STARTED WONDERING, WILL I EVER BE ABLE TO HAVE A PROPER CAREER? BEYOND FIGHTING AND MAYHEM, THAT IS. MY BOSS CAN DEDICATE HIMSELF TO HIS JOB AND AFFORD SHARP SUITS.

BEING THE SLAYER WON'T STOP YOU FROM HAVING A JOB.

NO, BUT IT STANDS IN THE WAY OF HAVING A CAREER. I WON'T EVER BE ABLE TO PUT ALL MY ENERGIES INTO ANYTHING OTHER THAN BEING THE SLAYER. THAT WILL ALWAYS BE THE PRIORITY.

IMAGINE IF I TRIED TO BE A DOCTOR. "I'M SORRY, NURSE, THIS PATIENT'S SUCKING CHEST WOUND WILL JUST HAVE TO WAIT. I HAVE TO WRESTLE THE LICH-CRAB OF CENTRAL ANGOLA."

Well, PERHAPS MEDICINE ISN'T FOR YOU. THERE ARE LESS DEMANDING FIELDS.

IS MY FUTURE IN RETAIL? I HAVE VISIONS OF MYSELF IN TEN YEARS' TIME, STILL SCRAPING BY ON MINIMUM WAGE, SERVING SLUSHIES AND RENTING MOVIES WHILE BEING THE SLAYER GETS ME SACKED FROM JOB AFTER POINTLESS JOB.

"...HELL ON ICE."

I CAN SUMMON THE SMALL FRY. NEXT TIME WILL BE A CALL UP FROM THE BIG LEAGUE. THEN THERE'LL BE NO MORE OF THIS DEAD-END FRANCHISE SLAVERY. I'LL HAVE A DEMON IN MY THRALL TO EARN MY FORTUNE FOR ME...

...I DIDN'T WANT ANYONE TO KNOW ABOUT MY SUCKY EMPLOYMENT BECAUSE OF GILES. THE FROSTY GREMLIN BLEW THAT IDEA--I HAD TO INFORM GILES ABOUT THE WEIRD STUFF.

OH, SEE HOW HE STRUMS THE BAR CHORDS?

OF COURSE, HE WENT BALLISTIC. WELL, AS BALLISTIC AS GILES CAN. I MANAGED TO PERSUADE HIM TO LET ME KEEP THE JOB, AS A LOOKOUT FOR OTHER MALL MONSTERS. SO, GILES AND ANGEL SEARCH FOR INFO, AND I MANAGE TO SNEAK AWAY TO REST MY ACHING FEET...AND HEART.

THE WAY HE SQUINTS WHEN HE TUNES HIS GUITAR.

...AND THAT'S WHEN I DECIDED TO HAVE THE SECOND HEAD ATTACHED. IT WENT WELL FOR AWHILE, BUT I DISCOVERED I WAS TALKING TO MYSELF ALL THE TIME, LIKE I'M DOING NOW.

NO, NO, I'M LISTENING THE SECOND HEAD FROM THE MALL? I KNOW, THEY'RE SO EXPENSIVE.

HEY, GUYS, WHASSUP?

THE USUAL-- MY LIFE SUCKS AND WILL'S GA-GA OVER HER GUITAR HERO.

BUFFY HAS A JOB AT THE MALL.

A WHAT?

THE DICTIONARY DEFINES IT AS: THE THING YOU DO WHEN DADDY DOESN'T GIVE YOU AN ALLOWANCE. I NEED A DRESS FOR THE DANCE, SO I HAVE TO WORK.

AHA! THE DANCE, *RIGHT?* 'CUZ OZ AND I ARE X-MAS SHOPPING IN THE MORNING. WE'RE GONNA BOND AT THE MALL, Y'KNOW, SCOPE THE CHICK ACTION, HANG AT THE ARCADE, AND BUY HIM A FLEA COLLAR.

WHAT, *ME*, NOT GO TO A SCHOOL DANCE? AS IF! AS THE MOST POPULAR GIRL IN SCHOOL, IT'S MY DUTY TO ATTEND.

LISTEN, GUYS, THERE WAS SOME KIND OF GREMLIN THING IN THE MALL TONIGHT. GILES SAYS WE SHOULD BE CAREFUL AROUND HERE.

THE DAY THEY TAKE AWAY MY RIGHT TO SHOP IS THE DAY I DIE. THEY'LL HAVE TO WRENCH MY CREDIT CARD FROM MY COLD, DEAD HANDS.

LET'S TAKE A MOMENT TO SAVOR THAT IMAGE.

WELL, CORDELIA, IF YOU WANT MY GIFTS, YOU HAVE TO ACCOMPANY ME TO THE DANCE.

I GUESS AS A CHARITABLE CONTRIBUTION TO THE LESS POPULAR.

YOU COULD SHOP FOR A VERY EXPENSIVE DRESS THAT'LL STUN EVERYONE, SOMETHING SO EYE-CATCHING THEY DON'T EVEN NOTICE XANDER'S THERE.

OKAY, NOW SHE'S GOING WITH ME.

OF COURSE! SOMETHING SMALL BUT PRECIOUS-- THIS WEATHER IS STIFLING.

DON'T LET YOUR CONSUMING-OBSESSED MINDS FORGET THE DANGER AT THE MALL.

SO, I FIGURE I'LL BUY CORDY'S PRESENT FROM TARGET AND BLOW THE CHANGE IN THE ARCADE.

Art by RANDY GREEN and RICK KETCHAM

...I HAD TO RETURN THE PERSONAL ORGANIZER BECAUSE THERE WERE ONLY TWENTY ADDRESS PAGES. THE CHECK-OUT GIRL, OR I SHOULD SAY CHECK-OUT HAG, WAS ALL "NO CASH REFUNDS"...

WHAT DID SHE SAY?

NOTHING... EXCEPT "BE CAREFUL, YOU DON'T WANT TO MAKE HER ANGRY."

...I TOLD HER TWENTY PAGES MIGHT BE SUFFICIENT FOR HER, BUT FOR SOMEONE AS POPULAR AS MYSELF...

CORDELIA!

WE APPRECIATE THE RUN-DOWN ON THE POST-CHRISTMAS GIFT RETURN SITUATION.

EX-CUUSE ME.

SO, WHAT EXACTLY HAPPENED THAT NIGHT?

LIKE I TOLD YOU, WILL CALLS ME UP IN THE MIDDLE OF THE NIGHT, ALL FREAKED OUT. OZ HAS BUSTED OUT OF HIS MANACLES AND IS AN AMERICAN WEREWOLF IN SUNNYDALE.

SO, GILES AND I GO OUT TO BRING THE STRAY HOME. ONLY OZ IS NOT SO ACCOMODATING, y'know?

WHADDYA. MEAN, "NOT SO ACCOMODATING"?

WE'RE DOING A LION-TAMER-TANGO. MY HEAD'S HALF IN HIS MOUTH AND I'M TRYING TO AVOID RECEIVING A HAIRCUT. SOME FORCE WAS NEEDED TO RESTRAIN HIM UNTIL GILES SCORED WITH THE TRANQUILIZER DART.

WHEN THE MOON GOES DOWN, HE'S A LITTLE BANGED UP?

YEAH, I APOLOGIZED AND EVERYTHING. OZ WAS COOL ABOUT IT, HE WAS JUST GLAD NO ONE GOT...

...EATEN?

Uh-huh. BUT NOW WILLOW WILL BARELY EVEN SPEAK TO ME. SHE ACTUALLY BELIEVES I ENJOYED BEATING UP ON OZ. I WAS ONLY STOPPING SOMETHING AWFUL FROM HAPPENING.

BEE-BEEP BEE-BEEP

GILES.

OH, MAN! WHY CAN'T VAMPS JUST STAY HOME, TOO BLOATED FROM XMAS FOOD AND TV RERUNS TO DO ANYTHING? JUST LIKE THE REST OF US.

TRAWLING THE SALES FOR BARGAINS CAN'T KEEP 'EM DISTRACTED FOREVER.

I CAME IN TO COLLECT SOME RESEARCH MATERIALS, ONLY TO DISCOVER WE'D HAD A VISITOR.

SOMEONE JUST COULDN'T WAIT 'TIL SCHOOL TO READ THE LATEST JACKIE COLLINS BEST SELLER.

I'M AFRAID THE CONTENTS OF THESE BOOKS ARE EVEN MORE FRIGHTENING THAN MS. COLLINS' CREATIONS.

YOU'VE OBVIOUSLY NEVER READ ONE OF HER "NOVELS".

WITCHCRAFT AND DEMONOLOGY, THE IDIOT'S GUIDE TO ALCHEMY -- NOT QUITE SEX AND SHOPPING MATERIAL.

ALCHEMY AND WITCHCRAFT? I CAN CROSS-REFERENCE WITH THE COMPUTER FILES, TRY AND IDENTIFY ANY BOOKS THAT MIGHT BE MISSING.

GOOD IDEA.

IS SOMETHING HAPPENING THAT I SHOULD KNOW ABOUT?

LET ME TALK TO WILLOW.

C'MON, GILES! ISN'T IT OBVIOUS? WILLOW IS UPSET BECAUSE BUFFY'S A MONTH OVERDUE ON A LIBRARY BOOK. D'UH.

AH, YES, OF COURSE. HOW SILLY OF ME NOT TO NOTICE.

ELSA DENSE HAS SPOKEN.

WHOK

URRRR

BUFFY, BE CAREFUL! THAT'S A PRICELESS EDITION OF THE *MALLEUS MALLEFICARUM.*

GRROOWWWL

WELL, I GUESS IT'LL MAKE A NICE COASTER?

ROWWLLLL

SIT, BOY, SIT?

YELPPPPP

THUNK

I GOT IT!

ARE YOU HURT, ANYTHING BROKEN?

JUST LET ME RECOVER FROM AN O.D. OF DOGGY BREATH. *YEESH!*

WHAT'S WITH THE SHARPSHOOTING?

SOMEONE HAD TO DO SOMETHING WHILE YOU GEEKS WERE STANDING AROUND WATCHING BUFFY GET MAULED.

HE WAS ONE SMART MUTT. HE HEADED STRAIGHT FOR THE ALCHEMY SECTION.

MAYBE HE WANTED TO KNOW HOW TO TURN LEAD INTO DOG FOOD.

MAKE MY DAY, PUNK!

IT'S RATHER A COINCIDENCE TO HAVE TWO BREAK-INS IN ONE NIGHT. ONE OF THE PERPETRATORS BEING A RABID MONGREL MAKES IT ESPECIALLY INTRIGUING.

I'LL SEARCH FOR ANY MENTION OF BLACK DOGS IN FOLKLORE.

AND I'LL TRY TO FIND THE BIGGEST CHOKE-CHAIN IN TOWN.

IF WE FOCUS OUR ATTENTION ON THE AREAS OF WITCHCRAFT AND ALCHEMY, WE MAY FIND OUR ANSWERS QUICKER.

CAN YOU GET THIS IN POWDER BLUE? IT WOULD ACCESSORIZE PERFECTLY WITH MY BODY SUIT.

YOU HAVE A BODY SUIT?

I KNOW MY EVIL EYE FROM MY PHILOSOPHER'S STONE, TOO MUCH ABOUT TRANSMUTATION, AND IF THERE WERE MIDTERMS ON THE OCCULT, I'D BE ON THE HONOR ROLL.

≁URGH≁ IT'S AWFUL, THE WAY THEY'D TEST IF YOU WERE A WITCH, BY THROWING YOU IN THE RIVER.

I KNOW. IF YOU SUNK YOU WERE INNOCENT, BUT DEAD. IF YOU FLOATED, YOU WERE STONED TO DEATH. *TERRIBLE.*

THAT WAS BAD, BUT THEY MADE YOU WEAR A SACK! THAT'S BARBARIC!

PARANORMAL POP-QUIZ TIME. WHAT IS TYROMANCY?

DIVINATION BY THE COAGULATION OF CHEESE.

DAMN. YOU'RE GOOD!

WILL YOU PLEASE ASK BUFFY TO HAND ME VOLUME TWO OF THE *"DICTIONAIRE INFERAL"?*

YOU COULD ASK HER YOURSELF. SHE IS SITTING RIGHT NEXT TO ME.

≁SIGH≁

OZ, WOULD YOU PLEASE ASK WILLOW TO QUIT ACTING LIKE A THIRD-GRADER?

OZ, *PLEASE* ASK BUFFY IF SHE INTENDS TO MAKE ME STOP. AFTER ALL, I WOULDN'T WANT TO CROSS THE *SLAYER*.

OZ, PLEASE INFORM WILLOW, IN CASE SHE ISN'T AWARE--SARCASM IS THE LOWEST FORM OF WIT.

WILL YOU TWO STOP THIS INFERNAL NONSENSE AT ONCE? OR DO I HAVE TO MAKE YOU BOTH STAND IN A CORNER? OR ARE WE GOING TO FIND THIS HELLHOUND AT LOOSE IN SUNNYVALE?

I FOUND MENTION OF A "BLACK-DOG CURSE" IN A TRANSLATION OF "DE PRAESIGIS DAEMONUM."

I NOTICED A "HELLHOUND CURSE" IN RECORDS CALLED "WITCH TRIALS OF THE NEW WORLD."

THAT IS INTERESTING. I FOUND REFERENCE TO TWO WITCHES WHOSE FAMILIAR WAS A BLACK DOG, IN TRIAL RECORDS FROM NEW ENGLAND.

MARIANA AND BEN JOHNSON? BURNT AT THE STAKE FOR WITCHCRAFT?

LET ME SEE..."ACCUSED OF MISCHIEF BY NATHANIEL FILMER, SON OF JUDGE ROBERT FILMER." THE WITCHES CURSED NATHANIEL AS THEY BURNT AT THE STAKE. FEARING THE HEX, HE DISAPPEARED AND WAS NEVER SEEN AGAIN.

...CURSES...
HURRY, HURRY...
CURSES...

YOU COULD
HAVE TAKEN
THE MAINTENANCE
ELEVATOR. LESS
TAXING.

Art by ARTHUR ADAMS and JOYCE CHIN

New Kid
on the Block

chapter 1

THIS COULD ONLY BE FUN ON SCHOOL TIME. THIS TOWN NEEDS MORE TEACHER-TRAINING DAYS!

CAN YOU TWO CUT TO THE GROUP HUG AND FINISH YOUR "EXTREME" BONDING SESSION ALREADY?

YOU RULE, NO ONE ELSE EVEN LIKES SKATING! I NEVER EXPECTED THE NEW GIRL TO BE SO COOL!

HEY! HOW LONG AM I GOING TO BE THE NEW GIRL? IT'S BEEN A COUPLA WEEKS SINCE I STARTED HERE.

MAN, MY BEARINGS ARE SHOT.

HEY, BUG-EYED BOY! YOU'RE DROOLING ON MY GUCCI SHOES.

IT'S A PAVLOVIAN RESPONSE, CORDELIA. THERE IS NO CURE.

SO, HOW ARE WE GOING TO USE THIS TREASURED DOWNTIME?

I'D SUGGEST SHOPPING IF I WANTED YOUR UNIVERSAL SCORN. HOWEVER, AS WE ARE THE "SLACKER GENERATION," I SUGGEST WE SHOULD DO NOTHING.

I'D LIKE TO PUNCH THE MIDDLE-AGED SOCIOLOGIST IDIOT WHO CAME UP WITH THAT! I NEVER GET TIME TO "SLACK"!

SPEAKING OF WHICH...

HEY, IT'S THAT LIBRARIAN GUY AGAIN. WHAT'S HIS DEAL, WHY'S HE ALWAYS ON BUFFY'S CASE?

HE'S JUST A CLOSE... FAMILY FRIEND. *RIGHT*, GUYS?

YEAH, A KIND OF PERSONAL TUTOR.

CUTTING CLASS, GILES? I'M SHOCKED, YOU BEING THE ROLE MODEL AND ALL.

I WANTED TO REMIND YOU THAT JUST BECAUSE YOU HAVE TODAY OFF, I DO NOT WANT YOU TO MISS TOMORROW'S PATROL.

COMING FROM A TRUANT THAT'S PRETTY RICH. HAVE I EVER MISSED A SATURDAY-NIGHT PATROL? IT'S THE ENTERTAINMENT HIGHLIGHT OF MY WEEK.

I SEE YOU'VE FOUND A FRIEND IN THE NEW GIRL. YOU HAVEN'T TOLD HER...

SHE HAS A NAME, GILES. CYNTHIA IS REALLY NICE, AND *NO*, SHE DOESN'T KNOW ABOUT MY EXTRACURRICULAR ACTIVITIES.

I'M GLAD TO HEAR SHE'S NOT A MEMBER OF THE "GANG. A SLAYER MUST NEVER LET DOWN HER GUARD.

I KNOW, A SLAYER MUST ALWAYS BE SUSPICIOUS, RIGHT?

YEAH, JUST A FEW OVERDUE BOOKS. SO...

EVERYTHING OKAY?

"...WHAT'S NEXT?"

...Y'KNOW, WE SHOULD DO SOMETHING REALLY FUN.

BUSMAN'S HOLIDAY FOR BUFFY.

BLAM BLAM BLAM

SPLAT

AIEEEE!

DIE, DIE, DIEEE!

BLAM BLAM BLAM SCHLUP... ARRGHHHH!

I DUNNO, MAYBE A MOVIE. ANY IDEAS?

DEAD, AGAIN.

GAME
INSERT COIN TO CONTINUE

Y'KNOW THIS MIGHT SOUND WEIRD, BUT IT'S SOMETHING I HAVEN'T DONE IN YEARS. IT'D BE SO MUCH FUN, I ALWAYS LOVED THEM AS A KID...

OH REALLY, WHAT?

...MY GUN WAS BUSTED. THAT'S THE ONLY REASON...

YEAH, I'VE HEARD THAT EXCUSE BEFORE.

BACK TO YOUR WEIRD IDEA.

I THOUGHT IT'D BE COOL TO HAVE A SLUMBER PARTY?

A SLUMBER PARTY? AWESOME IDEA!

A SLUMBER PARTY SOUNDS GREAT! MY PARENTS ARE AWAY THIS WEEKEND, SO WE COULD ALL HANG OUT AT MY PLACE.

WE SHOULD INVITE ANOTHER FRIEND EACH. TO REACH THAT PERFECT SLUMBER PARTY NUMBER.

SO, DO WE ALL HAVE TO WEAR LIKE, OUR "JAMMIES" AND STUFF?

Uh, sure--

NO GUYS ALLOWED!

WHAT DO YOU MEAN? IS THAT SOME IRON LAW LAID DOWN BY "YM" MAGAZINE? THIS IS THE NINETIES, I'LL SUE FOR SEX DISCRIMINATION!

C'MON, I'M JUST LIKE ONE OF THE GIRLS.

LISTEN TO ALLY MC BEAL!

XANDER, MY FRIEND. I HAVE TO STEP IN HERE TO PREVENT FURTHER DAMAGE TO THE REPUTATION OF THE "SENSITIVE GUYS" CLUB.

I'M GOING TO THAT PARTY...

C'MON, OZ. BACK ME UP HERE. WHY SHOULD WE BE EXCLUDED FROM THE FUN?

:SIGH: THE ONLY FUN YOU'LL MISS IS SEEING LEONARDO DI CAPRIO'S FACE FREEZE-FRAMED ON THE VCR FOR HOURS ON END.

...SATURDAY NIGHT HOCKEY WITH THE L.A. KINGS...

LET'S SEE... FLASHLIGHT, CHECK.

I'LL GIVE THEM ONE LAST CHANCE.

OFF THE HOOK. WELL, IF THEY DON'T INVITE ME, I'M JUST GOING TO HAVE TO...

...INVITE MYSELF!

WHAT IS THIS? FROM K-MART'S BUDGET STORE?

I THOUGHT THEY LOOKED CUTE AND...

I WAS REFERRING TO YOUR CHOICE IN SNACKS, BUT NOW THAT YOU MENTION IT...

I'M SURPRISED YOU EVEN KNOW WHAT THE INSIDE OF A KITCHEN LOOKS LIKE.

I DON'T NEED TO. THAT'S WHY WE HIRE HELP!

SO! YOU ADMIT YOU NEED HELP?

"HOW CAMEST THOU HITHER, TELL ME, AND WHEREFORE?..."

"...THE ORCHARD WALLS ARE HIGH AND HARD TO CLIMB, AND THE PLACE OF DEATH, CONSIDERING WHO THOU ART, IF ANY OF MY KINSMEN FIND THEE HERE."

"WITH LOVE'S LIGHT WINGS DID I O'ERPERCH THESE WALLS. FOR STONY LIMITS CANNOT HOLD LOVE OUT..."

"...AND WHAT LOVE...CAN DO THAT...DARES...LOVE ATTEM--"

Y'KNOW, MAYBE ENG. LIT. ISN'T QUITE THE SUBJECT TO KEEP OUR MINDS OFF... YOU KNOW.

Ur-hmm! I HAD NOTHING BUT POETRY ON MY MIND!

IF GUYS SPENT ALL THEIR TIME PAINTING EACH OTHERS' TOENAILS INSTEAD OF WATCHING FOOTBALL, IT'D THROW OUR ENTIRE CULTURE INTO A TAILSPIN TO OBLIVION.

WE HAVE A VISITOR.

SO, IT'S A SLUMBER PARTY AT TEN? Y'KNOW, IN ALL MY YEARS, I'VE NEVER ATTENDED A SLUMBER PARTY.

THAT'S BECAUSE YOU'RE A GUY. GUYS HAVE MONDAY NIGHT FOOTBALL BONDING SESSIONS, IT'S AN ENTIRELY DIFFERENT ATMOSPHERE.

THAT'S CYNTHIA. SHE MUST BE HEADING TO THE PARTY. THOSE GUYS KINDA LOOK WEIRD.

THE NEW GIRL, DOES SHE HAVE A DEATH WISH?

RUN, CYNTHIA! *RUN!*

WHA--?

RUN!

AIEEEEEE!

NOOOO VOOOO!!

RARRRGHH!

TIME FOR A LITTLE SPRING-CLEANING.

=sob sob=

FIRST, GET RID OF UNWANTED GUESTS.

NEVER PICK ON MY BOYFRIEND!

OOMPH!

CRUNCH

GNNNNN!

;Sob Sob;- B-BUFFY?

CYNTHIA? ARE YOU HURT?

N-NO, I DON'T THINK SO. I MAY BE MENTALLY TRAUMATIZED, BUT...

IT HAPPENS TO US ALL AT SOME POINT. THIS IS THE REAL SUNNYDALE, CYNTHIA. YOU JUST HAVE TO DEAL.

BUT, WHO WERE THOSE GUYS? HOW DID YOU KNOW THEY WANTED TO HURT ME?

MUGGERS TEND TO HANG AROUND THESE PLACES.

THEY WEAR MASKS AND EVERYTHING, SO YOU CAN'T IDENTIFY THEM.

THEY SEEMED KIND OF VICIOUS FOR MUGGERS. THEIR MASKS SURE DID LOOK REAL!

WELL...THIS TOWN'S FULL OF FANCY DRESS-TYPE STORES. Y'CAN GET HOLD OF ALL KINDS OF FREAKY STUFF.

REALLY?

WELL, SUNNYDALE IS AN UNUSUAL PLACE.

SO I'M BEGINNING TO REALIZE.

SO WHERE'S YOUR BROODING BUT GORGEOUS TAG-TEAM PARTNER?

ANGEL! I'D FORGOTTEN. WELL, HE'S KINDA SHY.

WHERE'D YOU LEARN TO FIGHT LIKE THAT?

JANUARY SALES.

I'LL GET MORE SODA.

CAN YOU CALL FOR PIZZA WHILE YOU'RE UP? HERE'S THE ORDER. REMEMBER, NO ANCHOVIES FOR CORDELIA.

YIKES!

CRREAKKK

ERRR. MAYBE THIS WASN'T SUCH A GREAT IDEA.

FRESH SODA, SHOULD ANYONE WANT IT.

DID YOU MAKE THE PIZZA ORDER OKAY?

I'M ALL LEO'D OUT.

DON'T WORRY, SUPPER WILL BE SERVED REAL SOON.

YOU KNOW WHAT WOULD BE REALLY FUN TO DO BEFORE WE GET THE EATS?

SPOOKY TRUTH OR DARE.

WHAT'S THE "SPOOKY" PART?

WE SWITCH OFF ALL THE LIGHTS IN THE HOUSE AND PLAY IT IN THE DARK!

...I CAN'T DIVULGE THAT INFORMATION. I'LL HAVE TO TAKE THE DARE.

AWWW, SPOILSPORT.

DING DONG

MUST BE PIZZA ALREADY.

YOU GUYS CARRY ON, I'LL BE BACK IN A MINUTE.

WOW! YOU WERE QUICK. COME ON IN, I'LL TRY TO SCRAPE TOGETHER A TIP.

New Kid
on the Block
chapter 2

GURGLE

OKAY, STOMACH. YOU WIN. LET'S FIND THE KITCHEN.

HEY, SAVE SOME ICE CREAM FOR ME.

DOWN, BOY!

BUFFY!

GRARRR!

NO PROBLEM.

KER-RASH

HURRY IT UP, GUYS. I DON'T HAVE ALL NIGHT.

WILLOW?

AIEEEEEE!

XANDER! WHAT ARE YOU DOING?

SOOTHING MY PERFORATED EARDRUMS!

I MEAN, WHAT ARE YOU DOING STALKING AROUND INSIDE MY HOUSE?

I... I HAD A VISION.

DID IT INVOLVE BUFFY IN HER UNDERWEAR?

PLEASE DRAG YOUR MIND OUT OF THE GUTTER, WILLOW.

YIKES.

ANYWAY, WE'VE GOTTA GET EVERYONE OUTTA HERE. BUFF'S CLEARING OUT A VAMP INFESTATION IN YOUR KITCHEN.

DARN IT. I WARNED MOM TO SCRUB BEHIND THE STOVE.

GLURK!

PTHUNK

ANGEL! WHERE'D YOU GO? WHAT HAPPENED?

I TRACKED DOWN THAT STRAY VAMP AND HE SPILLED THE BEANS. I'M WISE TO THE SCAM-- I'VE SEEN IT BEFORE.

SCAM?

THE GANG OF VAMPIRES YOU DUSTED WERE NEW TO THE AREA. THEY SIDLE IN AND PUT DOWN ROOTS WITH THE HELP OF YOUR NEW FRIEND, CYNTHIA.

SHE'S PART OF THE BITEY POSSE?

SHE'S THE MORTAL DAUGHTER OF THE HEAD VAMPIRE. HER STING IS TO MOVE INTO A NEW SCHOOL, MAKE FRIENDS WITH A "BOOKISH" TYPE AND PLAN A LAVISH SLUMBER PARTY.

WHICH THE VAMPS CRASH AND SCARF THE INSTANT FEAST.

THEN THEY EITHER WAIT AROUND OR MOVE ON TO A NEW TOWN.

THERE WAS NO BOSS VAMPIRE OUT OF THE BUNCH I TOASTED. SO WHERE IS HE AND HIS LOVING DAUGHTER--?

AIEEEEE

EEEEK!

THIS MEANS DADDY-VAMP WASN'T THE LEADER AFTER ALL.

SHE'S THE DAUGHTER FROM HELL.

SHE'S NOT A HAPPY BUNNY.

GRARRHHH

NO WONDER! IT CAN'T BE EASY FINDING FASHIONABLE CLOTHES FOR SOMEONE HER SIZE.

WHAT'RE THE ODDS OF HER BEING ON A VEGETARIAN HEALTH KICK?

DEMONS ARE INTO INSTANT GRATIFICATION.

LOOK FOR THESE BUFFY THE VAMPIRE SLAYER
TRADE PAPERBACKS FROM TITAN BOOKS

THE DUST WALTZ
Brereton • Gomez • Florea
80-page color paperback
ISBN: 1-84023-057-6 **£7.99**

THE REMAINING SUNLIGHT
Watson • Bennett • Ketcham
80-page color paperback
ISBN: 1-84023-078-9 **£7.99**

THE ORIGIN
Golden • Brereton • Bennett • Ketcham
80-page color paperback
ISBN: 1-84023-105-X **£7.99**

UNINVITED GUESTS
Watson • Gomez • Florea
104-page color paperback
ISBN: 1-84023-140-8 **£8.99**

SUPERNATURAL DEFENSE KIT
Watson • Richards • Pimentel
30-page color hard cover
comes with golden colored cross,
"claddagh" ring, and vial of "holy water"
ISBN: 1-84023-165-3 **£19.99**

All publications are available through most good bookshops or direct from our
mail-order service at Titan Books. For a free graphic-novels catalogue or to
order, telephone 01858 433 169 with your credit-card details or contact
Titan Books Mail Order, Bowden House, 36 Northampton Road,
Market Harborough, Leics, LE16 9HE, quoting reference BUG/GN.

www.buffy.com

STAR WARS

CRIMSON EMPIRE
Richardson • Stradley
Gulacy • Russell
160-page color paperback
ISBN: 1-84023-006-1

EPISODE 1—
THE PHANTOM MENACE
Gilroy • Damaggio • Williamson
112-page color paperback
ISBN: 1-84023-025-8

THE LAST COMMAND
Baron • Biukovic • Shanower
144-page color paperback
ISBN: 1-84023-007-X

MARA JADE:
BY THE EMPEROR'S HAND
Zahn • Stackpole • Ezquerra
144-page color paperback
ISBN: 1-84023-011-8

TALES OF THE JEDI: THE
GOLDEN AGE OF THE SITH
Anderson • Gossett
Carrasco • Heike • Black
Beckett • Woch
144-page color paperback
ISBN: 1-84023-000-2

X-WING ROGUE SQUADRON:
THE WARRIOR PRINCESS
Stackpole • Tolson
Nadeau • Ensign
96-page color paperback
ISBN: 1-85286-997-6

X-WING ROGUE SQUADRON:
REQUIEM FOR A ROGUE
Stackpole • Strnad • Erskine
112-page color paperback
ISBN: 1-84023-026-6

X-WING ROGUE SQUADRON:
IN THE EMPIRE'S SERVICE
Stackpole • Nadeau • Ensign
96-page color paperback
ISBN: 1-84023-008-8

X-WING ROGUE SQUADRON:
BLOOD AND HONOR
Stackpole • Crespo
Hall • Johnson
96-page color paperback
ISBN: 1-84023-010-X

ALIENS

FEMALE WAR
(formerly *Aliens: Earth War*)
Verheiden • Kieth
112-page color paperback
ISBN: 1-85286-784-1

GENOCIDE
Arcudi • Willis • Story
112-page color paperback
ISBN: 1-85286-805-8

HARVEST
(formerly *Aliens: Hive*)
Prosser • Jones
128-page color paperback
ISBN: 1-85286-838-4

LABYRINTH
Woodring • Plunkett
136-page color paperback
ISBN: 1-85286-844-9

NIGHTMARE ASYLUM
(formerly *Aliens: Book Two*)
Verheiden • Beauvais
112-page color paperback
ISBN: 1-85286-765-5

OUTBREAK
(formerly *Aliens: Book One*)
Verheiden • Nelson
168-page color paperback
ISBN: 1-85286-756-6

ROGUE
Edginton • Simpson
112-page color paperback
ISBN: 1-85286-851-1

STRONGHOLD
Arcudi • Mahnke • Palmiotti
112-page color paperback
ISBN: 1-85286-875-9

ALIENS VS PREDATOR

ALIENS VS PREDATOR
Stradley • Norwood • Warner
Story • Campanella
176-page color paperback
ISBN: 1-85286-413-3

THE DEADLIEST
OF THE SPECIES
Claremont • Guice • Barreto
320-page color paperback
ISBN: 1-85286-953-4

WAR
various
200-page color paperback
ISBN: 1-85286-703-5

BATMAN VS PREDATOR

BATMAN VS PREDATOR
Gibbons • Kubert • Kubert
96-page color paperback
ISBN: 1-85286-446-X

BATMAN VS PREDATOR II:
BLOODMATCH
Moench• Gulacy • Austin
136-page color paperback
ISBN: 1-85286-667-5

BATMAN VS PREDATOR III:
BLOOD TIES
Dixon • Damaggio
136-page color paperback
ISBN: 1-85286-913-5

BUFFY THE VAMPIRE
SLAYER

THE DUST WALTZ
Brereton • Gomez
80-page color paperback
ISBN: 1-84023-057-6

THE REMAINING SUNLIGHT
Watson • Van Meter
Bennett • Ross • Ketcham
88-page color paperback
ISBN: 1-84023-078-9

THE ORIGIN
Golden • Brereton
Bennett • Ketcham
80-page color paperback
ISBN: 1-84023-105-X

UNINVITED GUESTS
Watson • Brereton
Gomez • Florea
96-page color paperback
ISBN: 1-84023-140-8

PREDATOR

BIG GAME
Arcudi • Dorkin • Gil
112-page color paperback
ISBN: 1-85286-454-0

COLD WAR
Verheiden • Randall • Mitchell
112-page color paperback
ISBN: 1-85286-576-8

KINDRED
Lamb • Tolson
112-page color paperback
ISBN: 1-85286-908-9

VARIOUS

BATMAN/ALIENS
Marz • Wrightson
128-page color paperback
ISBN: 1-85286-887-2

PREDATOR VS
JUDGE DREDD
Wagner • Alcatena
80-page color paperback
ISBN: 1-84023-021-5

TARZAN VS PREDATOR
AT THE EARTH'S CORE
Simonson • Weeks
104-page color paperback
ISBN: 1-85286-888-0